★DOVER★
CHILDREN'S THRIFT CLASSICS

The Glass Mountain
and Other Polish Fairy Tales

Translated from the Polish and adapted by
ELSIE BYRDE

Illustrated by Marty Noble

DOVER PUBLICATIONS, INC.
Mineola, New York

DOVER CHILDREN'S THRIFT CLASSICS
EDITOR OF THIS VOLUME: JULIE NORD

Copyright

Copyright © 2000 by Dover Publications, Inc.
All rights reserved under Pan American and International Copyright Conventions.

Published in Canada by General Publishing Company, Ltd., 30 Lesmill Road, Don Mills, Toronto, Ontario.

Bibliographical Note

The Glass Mountain and Other Polish Fairy Tales, first published by Dover Publications, Inc. in 2000, is a new anthology containing the unabridged texts of six stories selected from *The Polish Fairy Book,* as published by T. Fisher Unwin Limited, London, in 1925. The introductory note and illustrations have been specially created for this edition.

Library of Congress Cataloging-in-Publication Data

Byrde, Elsie.
  [Polish fairy tales]
  The Glass mountain and other Polish fairy tales / translated from the Polish and adapted by Elsie Byrde ; illustrated by Marty Noble.
      p. cm.
  Originally published: Polish fairy tales, 1925.
  ISBN 0-486-41306-3 (pbk.)
    1. Fairy tales—Poland. I. Title.

GR195 .B97 2000
398.2'09438—dc21

00-057100

Manufactured in the United States of America
Dover Publications, Inc., 31 East 2nd Street, Mineola, N.Y. 11501

Note

Early in the twentieth century, Elsie Byrde took it upon herself to translate and adapt some of the wealth of folk tales originating with the people of Poland. She combed through original sources in the University Library, Warsaw, and found there many treasures: stories full of humor, humanity, fantastical creatures and events, and amazing inventiveness. Reprinted here are some of the loveliest of the Polish tales she published. They boast such enchanting characters as a magic wolf who can turn himself into anything at all—a beautiful bird, a princess— a princess who can turn herself into a bee, and a horse whose advice is always wise and whose magic powers can right all wrongs. As Elsie Byrde wrote, "you never know whether the blackbird that whistles to you in the early morning, or the cow that gives you milk for breakfast, or the dog that wags his tail when you meet him in the road, is just a blackbird, a cow, or a dog—or is a fairy. Any one of them may be that, so it is a good thing to make friends with them all."

Contents

List of Illustrations

About Prince Surprise

THERE was once a king and queen who had been married for three whole years, yet had no heir, and that was a great grief to them. One day the king took leave of his queen and set off on a long journey through his kingdom.

After nearly nine months of absence as he was on his way home and quite near to the capital city, he passed through a lonely field, and, feeling very thirsty, sent his retainers to look for water. They searched in every direction for a whole hour, but returned without having found any.

Then the thirsty king himself rode over the length and breadth of the field, for he would not believe there was no spring to be found. And at last he came to a well which had a brand new bucket filled to the brim with fresh water, and on the water was floating a silver goblet ornamented with gold.

The king sprang down from his horse, and, leaning with his left hand on the curb, reached with his right for the goblet. But the cup, as though it had eyes and were alive, darted from his grasp to the one side and then floated again on the water. The king went on his knees and tried and tried, now with his left hand, now with his right, to catch the goblet, but it eluded him even when he strove with both hands to capture it, now diving down like a fish and then up to the surface.

"Bother the goblet!" said the king. "I'll drink without it."

And he stooped over the well and drank the water, which was clear as crystal and cold as ice—stooped until his long beard was wet through and under the water. His thirst quenched, he would have risen, but something held him fast by the beard.

He pulled and pulled but it held on. Then in an angry voice he cried, "Who is that holding me? Let go at once!"

"It is I," was the answer, "the King of the Underworld, Darkness the immortal, and I will not let you go until you promise to give me that of which you know nothing and do not expect to find on your return home."

The king looked down into the well and saw a huge head the size of a bucket with green eyes and a mouth opened from ear to ear. The monster clutched the king's beard with enormous lobster-like claws and laughed mockingly.

Thinking that what he knew nothing of and did not expect to find at home could not be of much importance, the king said to the monster, "Very well, I will give it to you." It burst out in fresh laughter, shot out fire, and disappeared. And with it went the well, goblet and all: the king found himself kneeling on the dry sand of a hill near a wood.

He got up, crossed himself, sprang on his horse, caught up with his suite, and they all rode on.

After a week or two they came to the city and rode up to the palace door. There stood the queen, holding a cushion in her hands, and on the cushion was bound with a swaddling cloth a baby that was beautiful as the full-moon.

"Alas!" moaned the king, "this is what I knew not of and did not expect to see!" And he wept bitterly. Everybody wondered, but none dared ask the reason of his tears. He took his son in his arms, looked long on the innocent little face, and carried him into the palace himself.

He stifled his grief and devoted himself to the affairs of his State, but the thought of King Darkness in the well never left him and he could not regain his former lightheartedness.

*There stood the queen, holding a cushion in her hands,
and on the cushion was bound with a swaddling cloth a baby
that was beautiful as the full-moon.*

Weeks, months, and years passed, and nobody came for the prince. He was named Surprise, and grew up happily to be a fine young man. And the king in time regained his spirits and finally forgot all that had happened in that lonely field. But alas! there was one who had not forgotten!

One day the prince, while hunting in the wood, got separated from his followers. He wandered far along the wilds alone, and suddenly there stood before him a monstrous old man.

"How are you, Prince Surprise?" said he.

"Who are you that asks?" replied the prince.

"Ah, that you will know later on," said the old man. "At present return to your father, give him my compliments, and tell him that I should like him to settle our account, for if he does not soon get quit of his debt he will bitterly regret it."

So saying, the monster disappeared. The prince rode back home and related his adventure to the king, his father, who turned pale as he heard it, and then made known his secret.

"Do not weep, Father," said the prince. "There is no great misfortune. I will make King Darkness renounce his claim on me."

Then the king gave him a coat of mail, a sword and a horse; the queen hung round his neck a cross of pure gold, and, both weeping, they embraced him tenderly and let him go.

He rode for a whole day, for two and for three days more, and at the end of the fourth, at sunset, he found himself on the seashore. Lying on the strand were twelve dresses, white as snow, such as maidens wear, but as far as eye could reach no living soul was to be seen except that twelve goslings were swimming near the water's edge. Wondering to whom the dresses could belong, he took one up in his hand. Then he let his horse go loose in a field, and he himself hid in the rushes and waited to see what would happen.

Just then the goslings, tired of playing on the water, swam to shore. Eleven of them ran each to a dress, stamped on the ground with its foot, and turned into a beautiful maiden. They dressed themselves quickly and ran off into a field together. The twelfth gosling, and the prettiest, did not venture to the land but stretched out its neck looking in every direction till it caught sight of the prince. Then it said in a human voice:

"Prince Surprise, I shall be grateful to you for giving me back my dress." The prince obediently laid the dress on the ground and modestly turned away. The gosling at once ran to it on the grass, transformed itself into a maiden, dressed quickly and stood before him, so young and so beautiful that never had he seen the like of her. Blushing, with downcast eyes, she gave him her white hand, saying in a sweet voice:

"Thank you, good Prince, for obeying me. I am the youngest daughter of King Darkness, who reigns over the Underworld, and those you saw with me are my eleven sisters. My father has been expecting you for a long while, and he is very angry because you have not come. But do not be sad or afraid, just do what I tell you. When you see him, fall on your knees, and, taking no notice of his shouts, his stampings and his threats, go up to him on them. What happens afterwards—you will see. And now let us go."

Saying this, she struck the ground with her little foot. The ground melted away, and they entered the kingdom of the Underworld, going straight to the palace, which was brighter than the sun and lighted up all around it.

The prince went in boldly. There sat the king in a shining crown, on his golden throne. His eyes flashed like green crystals and his hands were like lobster's claws. The prince fell on his knees, and taking no notice of the king's shouts, stampings, and threats, worked his way on them to the throne.

"You are lucky, young giddy-pate," said King Darkness, "to have succeeded in making me laugh." For indeed he was laughing heartily. "You may stay in my kingdom, but before I give you the full rights of a citizen you must submit to three tests. As it is now so late, you must wait till to-morrow to hear what they are."

The prince went to the room appointed for him and fell into a pleasant sleep. Early next morning King Darkness sent for him, and said:

"Now we shall see, Prince, what you can do. You must build me, overnight, a palace of pure marble. The windows must be of crystal, the roof of gold; around it must be a beautiful garden and in the garden a pond and a fountain. If you can do this you win my favour, if you fail I shall have you beheaded."

When he had heard this the prince went back to his room. He was sitting there, thinking gloomily that he must die, when a bee, buzzing outside on the window-pane, said:

"Please let me in!"

He opened the window, the bee flew in, and then turned into the youngest daughter of King Darkness.

"What are you thinking about, Prince?" she asked.

"I am thinking of how your father wants to take my life," he replied.

"Fear not!" said the princess, "sleep in peace, for when you get up to-morrow morning the palace will be there."

And so it was. At dawn the prince looked out and saw a much more beautiful palace than any he had ever seen. King Darkness, when he beheld it, could scarcely believe his eyes.

"You have won this time," he said. "But you must submit to another test. To-morrow my twelve daughters shall stand before you and if you do not guess rightly which is the youngest—off with your head!"

"How could I *not* know his youngest daughter?" thought the prince when back in his room. "There is no difficulty in that."

"So much," replied the princess, who had flown into the room again in the shape of a bee, "that unless I help you to recognize me you will not do so, for we are all so alike that even my father only knows us by our dresses."

"What am I to do?" asked the prince.

"This. Above the right eyebrow of the youngest daughter there will be a ladybird. Look well! Good-bye." And away she flew.

Next morning the king sent for the prince. The princesses stood side by side in his presence, all dressed alike. The prince looked, and marvelled to find them all so exactly alike. Once, twice, he walked past them without seeing the sign agreed upon. But the third time he cried:

"This one is the youngest!"

"However did you guess that?" asked King Darkness. "There must be some trick in it. I must try something else on your highness! Come back in three hours' time and give us another display of your cleverness. I will light a straw, and before it burns out you must make a pair of boots, or if you can't you shall perish."

The prince returned to his room very angry. He found the bee there before him.

"Why are you so upset, Prince?" it said.

"Have I not reason to be upset?" he replied. "Your father orders me to make a pair of boots for him—as if I were a cobbler!"

"And what will you do?"

"What am I to do? The boots I won't make, but I am not afraid of death. I can only die once."

"No, Prince," said she, "you shall not die. Either we shall be saved together or die together. We must run away: there is nothing else to be done."

Thus saying the princess spat on the window-pane, and the spittle froze at once. Then with the prince she left the room, locked the door after her, and threw the key to a distance. Then, taking hands, they set off up the mountain so quickly that in a moment they found themselves at the exact spot where they had entered the Underworld. There was the same sea, the same rushes and reeds, the same green field, and in the field was wandering the prince's horse, which, as soon as it had seen its owner, neighed loudly and ran up to him.

The prince lost no time: he sprang on the horse, the princess sprang up behind him, and away they flew like an arrow.

Now King Darkness grew tired of waiting for the prince and sent to ask why he did not come. When the servants found the door locked, they knocked, and the spittle answered from within in the prince's voice—"In a minute!"

They took this answer to the king. He waited and waited, but the prince did not come. He sent again, and his messengers, hearing the same answer—"In a minute!"— went back and gave it.

"What?" cried the king angrily. "Does he dare to joke with me? Go and force open the door and bring him here!"

The servants flew back, pushed with all their might, the door fell open, but there was no one there, and the spittle was splitting its sides with laughing.

The king nearly burst with rage, and commanded that all should fly in pursuit of the prince and not come back without him. They jumped into their saddles and galloped off.

Now Prince Surprise and the princess were speeding along when suddenly they heard the pounding of horses' feet behind them. The prince sprang down, laid his ear to the ground and said, "They are following us!"

"There is no time to be lost!" cried the princess, and turned herself into a river, the prince into a bridge, and the horse into a crow, and made the high road branch in three directions. The pursuers came galloping on, following the fresh tracks, but when they came to the bridge they stopped in bewilderment. So far traces could be seen but no farther, and the highway was separated into three roads. There was nothing else to be done, and they went back home.

When the king saw them return without the prince he screamed with rage. "They were the river and the bridge themselves," he roared. "How was it you did not guess that? Back you go, and don't show your faces without them."

So away they rode again.

"I hear the sound of horses' hoofs," whispered the princess. Prince Surprise sprang from the saddle, put his ear to the ground and cried:

"They are coming at full gallop!—and are close upon us!"

Immediately the prince, the princess, and the horse became a dark wood in which were roads, paths, and tracks without number, and along one of the roads galloped, so it seemed, two horsemen.

Following the fresh prints the servants reached the wood and galloped after the two riders. They galloped and galloped, seeing before them always a dense wood, a wide road, and two riders fleeing from them. At last they seemed to be catching up to them, when suddenly they disappeared and the wood with them, and the servants found themselves at the spot from whence they had set out in pursuit. So back they had to go to the king without the fugitives.

"A horse! a horse! I will go after them myself! They won't escape *me*!" shouted the king, boiling with rage; and away he flew.

"I think someone is after us," said the princess, "and that it is the king, my father, himself. But at the first church his kingdom ends, and he will not be able to follow us farther. Give me your golden cross."

The prince took off his tender mother's gift and gave it to the princess, who at once turned herself into a church, the prince into a priest, and the horse into a belfry. After awhile King Darkness came up to it.

"Hi, Monk!" he cried to the priest. "Did you see some travellers pass?"

"Only Prince Surprise and King Darkness's youngest daughter. They went in to see the church, gave money for a mass to be said for your health, and asked me to give you their compliments if you should ride by."

So the king went back home. And Prince Surprise and the princess rode along without fear of being pursued again.

Suddenly they saw before them a beautiful town, and the prince was seized with a great desire to visit it.

"Prince," said the princess, "don't go: my heart foresees some misfortune."

"I will only be gone a minute," replied the prince. "I will just look in and then we will go on."

"There is no difficulty about your going," she replied, "but only about coming back. However, if you *must* go, then go, and I will turn myself into a white stone and wait for you. But be careful, my dear, for the king and queen and their daughter will come out to meet you, and with them will be a lovely little boy, whom you must not kiss, for if you do you will forget me. I will wait on the road for three days, but if you are not back by then I shall die of despair."

The prince said he would be back before then, and went off to the town. The princess changed herself into a white stone and lay by the roadside. One day passed, two days passed, three days passed, and no prince! no prince!

Poor princess! The prince had not heeded her caution. The king and queen and their daughter came out to meet him, and with them the child, a curly-headed boy with eyes like stars, who ran straight up to the prince, and he, charmed with the beauty of the little one, neglected the warning, stooped and kissed him. As he did so his memory became clouded and he forgot the princess.

She lay there on the road in the form of a white stone for two days patiently, but when by the end of the third day the prince did not return she moaned grievously, and, turning herself into a cornflower, sprang among the corn that grew near the road.

"I will stay here by the roadside," she thought, "and perhaps some passer-by will pick me or trample me underfoot." And tears like dewdrops trembled on her blue petals.

Just then an old man, who was walking through the corn, spied the flower, and, charmed with its loveliness, he carefully uprooted it, carried it to his cottage, set it in a pot, and began to tend it.

And now wonder of wonders! From the time he brought the cornflower into his house strange things began to happen there. The old man would scarce be awake when all was cleaned and swept and not a speck of dust remained. At midday he came home from work to find dinner ready, the table set, and all he had to do was to sit down and eat. The old man wondered and wondered, but at last he became frightened and went to get advice from an acquaintance, who was a soothsayer.

"This must you do," advised the soothsayer. "Get up before the first blush of morn, before cockcrow, and watch to see what first stirs in the house. Whatever it is, cover it with a handkerchief, and you will see what next happens."

That night the old man did not close an eye. No sooner did the day begin to break than the cornflower got out of the flowerpot and began to flit about the room, to put things in order, to sweep and dust and light the stove. Then the old man sprang nimbly from his bed and threw a handkerchief over the flower as it was running about—and behold! there stood before him a beautiful maiden!

"What have you done?" she cried. "Why have you brought me back to life? My lover, Prince Surprise, has forgotten me! My life is hateful to me."

Then the old man said:

"Your lover, Prince Surprise, is to be married to-day. The wedding feast is ready and the guests are on their way."

The princess burst into tears, but after a moment she dried them, put on a smock-frock, and went as a village girl to the town.

She went to the royal kitchen, where a deal of bustle and business was going on. Putting on her most attractive manner, she went up to the cook and asked in a sweet voice:

"Dear sir, please do me a favour! Allow me to bake the wedding cake."

Now the cook was busy and his first thought was to send her packing, but when he looked at her the sharp words died in his mouth, and he answered kindly,

"Oh, my beauty of beauties, do whatever you like. I will myself carry your cake to the prince."

So she baked the cake, and when all the guests were seated at the table the cook himself set it on a silver dish before the prince. He was just about to cut it when, behold! a wonder came to pass before the eyes of the party such as had never been heard of! A grey and a white dove rose together from the cake. The grey dove fluttered about the table, and the white one cooed after him:

> Oh, my dearest, my grey dove,
> Do not fly from me, my love!
> Like the Prince Surprise, will you
> To your sweetheart prove untrue?

When Prince Surprise heard this cooing of the dove his lost memory came back suddenly. He sprang from his seat, flew to the door, and there outside it was his princess, who took his hand and ran with him quickly to the entrance of the palace. The horse stood there ready saddled.

To his horse leaped the prince, and with the princess before him away they flew and at last arrived safely at his father's kingdom. The king and queen received them with great joy, and gave them a wedding the like of which eye has not seen or ear heard of in this world.

Bogdynek

THERE was once a peasant and his wife who had been married many, many years and still had no child. But one day, long after they had given up hoping for one, a little boy was born to them. Now they were very poor, and their cupboard was quite empty when the time came for the christening.

"What shall we do about godparents?" said the old woman, "for no one will want to stand for him if there is no christening feast."

The old man wondered too: he scratched his head, wondered more, and scratched his head again. Then he got up, took down his staff, and put his hat on his head.

"I'll go and look for a couple of godfathers," he said. "Maybe on the road I shall come across those who will do." And he set off on the high road.

He had not gone more than a few miles when he met two very aged men. They had long white hair and beards.

"Where are you going, Neighbour?" they asked.

"I am going to look for godfathers for my son," replied the peasant.

"We will stand for him," said the two old men. "Go home and take your wife and child to the church, and we'll be there waiting for you." So the father went home to fetch his wife and child to the church, and the baby was christened and given the name of Bogdynek.

After the ceremony, when the godfathers took leave of the parents, the first godfather said: "You will find my present in the cupboard at home." And the second gave them a key, saying: "This is the key of the stable that you will find outside your cottage. Keep it safely until your son is of age. Then open the stable door and you will find *my* present." With that the two godfathers went their way.

The first thing the old couple did when they got home was to look in the cupboard, and there they found enough meal and grain to last them a lifetime. Fed on this the little boy became healthy and sturdy, and was the joy of his parents' hearts. He grew up to be as fine a young man as you could ever wish to see.

One day, when he was about twenty years old, he said to his parents: "The time has now come for me to see something of life. Give me your blessing and let me go out into the world." So the parents gave him their blessing and sent him on his way.

He had not gone far when his father remembered the key of the stable.

"Stop, stop, Son!" he cried after him. When he caught up with him Bogdynek was sitting on a stone, having a rest. He looked around and saw his father hobbling down the road and holding up a key.

"Come back, little son!" he cried. "Come back, for we had forgotten to open the stable door to see what your godfather left there for you."

They went back and opened the door. In the stall stood a splendid horse. Bogdynek took leave again of his parents, jumped on its back and rode away. Beyond the third forest and the third river they came to a green meadow in which there was no path. As he was riding through the grass he saw a beautiful white lily.

"Kneel down," he said to his horse, "and let me pick this lily."

"Don't pick it," said the horse, "it will bring misfortune."

"I must have it," replied Bogdynek. "I don't see what harm it can do to me."

"Very well, have your own way," said the horse, and knelt down, and Bogdynek picked the lily.

A little farther on he saw another lily, white and beautiful like the first.

"Kneel down," he said to the horse, "and let me pick that lily."

"Don't pick it," replied the horse, "it will bring misfortune."

"I picked the other one and nothing happened," said Bogdynek; "why should I not pick this one too?"

"Very well," said the horse, "have your own way." And he knelt down and Bogdynek picked the lily.

A little farther on he saw another lily, and again he told the horse to kneel down and let him pick it.

"Don't pick it," said the horse, "for it will only bring you misfortune."

But Bogdynek insisted, and, having gathered the flower, tied all three in his handkerchief and rode on. Across the meadow and down a broad high road they came to a city.

Bogdynek rode into the city, went to the king's palace, and asked to be taken into the army. The king, pleased with the look of him, gave him a place in his own battalion, and a room in the tower of the palace.

Every night, when Bogdynek went to his room, he took the three lilies out of his handkerchief and set them near the window. When he did so the whole room was lit up with a bright light.

One night a watchman saw this light and told the king.

"Hi, there!" called out the king, going upstairs, "do you want to set the whole palace on fire?"

Instead of answering, Bogdynek went down on one knee at the top of the staircase and presented one of the lilies to the king, who was so pleased with this graceful act that he promoted the young man on the spot.

Soon after this some soldiers, returning from a journey, brought news of a princess of great beauty who lived on an island in the midst of the sea. The king desired very much to see her. "Who is so faithful, so capable, and so strong as Bogdynek?" he said. "Go, then, Bogdynek, and fetch me this princess. If you return without her you must die."

Now it is no easy matter to carry off a princess bodily from an island in the midst of a sea. Bogdynek had no idea how to set about it. In despair he went to his horse for advice.

"Didn't I tell you not to pick the lilies?" said the horse. "I said 'Don't pick the lilies,' and you said 'I don't see what harm will come of it!' Now you see misfortune *has* come of it. However, I will tell you what to do. Go to the end of the crystal bridge, and there you will find a ship. Go on board, taking with you a band of musicians, for the princess dotes on music. Sail to the island, and on your way, if anyone asks for help, give it."

Bogdynek went to the end of the crystal bridge, which was forty miles long; found the ship and set sail with his band. They had not gone far when they came to a shore on which three dogs were fighting; they were not really dogs but three princes, who were bewitched and who were fighting for a kingdom. They called to Bogdynek to settle the dispute. Bogdynek stopped the ship, and said:

"My advice is that the eldest reigns first, after him the second prince, and then the youngest."

The dogs agreed that this was the best way by far of settling the matter. They thanked Bogdynek and said: "If ever we can help you let us know."

A little farther on he saw a griffin carrying a dead horse, which it was trying to get into its nest in the thicket, but the trees grew so densely that it was impossible for it to fly through with so bulky a prey. It called to Bogdynek to help it, and he, leaving the ship, cut down enough of the trees to clear a passage for the griffin to its nest. The griffin thanked him and said: "If ever I can help you let me know."

Farther on he saw a whale stranded on a sandy beach. The poor creature was dying of thirst and called to Bogdynek for help. He left the ship, came to the whale, and gave it such a push that it rolled over and over into the sea. Putting its head out of the water it said: "Thank you! And if ever I can help you let me know."

On and on he sailed till at last he came to the island where the princess lived. Bogdynek told the band to play its sweetest music. The princess pricked up her ears at the sound, listened at her window, and at last came down to the shore to find out who was playing. Charmed with Bogdynek's looks she invited him to the palace. They dined together, and afterwards she showed him over the island, which was full of interesting things. Then he in his turn invited her to look over his ship.

He bade the band play its loudest after she came on board, and she was so delighted with the music that she never noticed that the anchor had been weighed and that they were sailing away from the island. When at last she said she wanted to go home they were miles from shore.

She was so angry at having been tricked that she threw the key of the palace into the sea.

When they arrived the king was overjoyed: he fell violently in love with the princess and asked her to marry him then and there. But she said: "Not until you send for my palace and have it set down here."

"Go, Bogdynek," said the king, "and fetch the princess her palace."

Now, how ever was Bogdynek to carry a whole palace on his back! He went to the horse in despair to ask his advice.

"Didn't I tell you not to pick the lilies?" said the horse. "I said 'Don't pick the lilies,' and you said 'What harm can come of it?' and now you see what has happened! Yet I will advise you. Those can best help you whom you helped on your way to the island."

So Bogdynek went to the dogs and asked them to fetch the princess's palace. They went, and in a short time came back, dragging it after them, and then they set it in front of the king's palace.

"Now," said the king to the princess, "will you marry me? The palace is here."

*The princess pricked up her ears at the sound, listened at her window,
and at last came down to the shore to find out who was playing.*

"That's all very well," replied the princess, "but how can I go into it when the door is locked and the key is lost?"

"Bogdynek," said the king, "go and fetch the key of the palace for the princess."

Now how was Bogdynek to fetch a key that was lying at the bottom of the sea! But he did not go to the horse this time for advice, but to the whale for help. The whale called all the fishes in the sea together and told them to look for the key. At last it was found, and Bogdynek took it to the king.

"Now," said the king to the princess, "will you marry me?"

"Not until I have the killing and healing water," replied the princess, "from the wells that are guarded by seven witches."

"Go, Bogdynek," said the king, "and fetch the killing and healing water for the princess."

What was poor Bogdynek to do now? He had not the faintest idea where to find the wells. He thought of the griffin, but first he went to his good steed and told him all about it. He was very much afraid of another scolding, but this time all the horse said was, with a sigh: "What a pity it was you picked the lilies!" Then he told him to take two bottles and attach to each a long string, and then to get the griffin to carry him on its back over the wells. There he was to let down the bottles into the wells, the right-hand bottle into the killing water and the left-hand bottle into the healing water.

All this Bogdynek did. When he drew the bottles up the seven witches flew out and spat fire at him, but the griffin travelled so swiftly that before they could hurt him he was out of sight. So he brought the water for the princess.

"Well, Princess, will you marry me now?" asked the king.

"Not until Bogdynek's head is cut off," replied the princess.

The king called his axeman. "Chop off Bogdynek's head," he said, and off it went.

Then the princess laughed, and, taking the bottle of healing water, she poured some of it over the head, and at once it was joined to the body again so that you would never dream it had been cut off.

"Now, King, it is your turn!" said the princess. "Unless you let the axeman cut off *your* head there will be no marriage." The king at once ordered the axeman to chop off his head, thinking of course that the princess would pour the healing water over him as she had done over Bogdynek. But when the king's head was off she laughed heartily.

"Let him lie there and wait," she said. "Time enough to put his head on again when we are married, Bogdynek!" For she had determined to marry none but him. She sprinkled the killing water over the king for fear he might come to life before the wedding was safely over, and so they left him and went to church, and there they were married so tightly that no king could ever unmarry them.

The good horse, who was really a fairy, when he saw that Bogdynek's good fortune was certain, forgave him for having picked the lilies against his advice. Seeing that he was no longer needed he went back to Fairyland, carrying with him the grateful thanks of Bogdynek and his princess, who lived happily ever after.

The Prince and the Foundling

THERE was once a handsome young prince who had just said good-bye to his parents and was starting off for the wars at the head of his army, when an old minstrel came before the palace gates and began to sing and play. The prince ordered his army to wait a few minutes, for he dearly loved to hear a song. When the old man had ended his song, he began to tell fortunes. To one he told that he would die on the field of battle, to another that he would come back safe and sound, to another that he would be wounded, and so on.

"Well, and what have you to tell me?" asked the prince.

"Your resplendent Highness will come home triumphant," answered the old minstrel.

"And what else?" asked the prince. "Perhaps you can tell me when I shall be married and who the princess will be."

"Your Highness will be married within a year," replied the minstrel, "but to no princess. Your resplendent Highness will marry a poor orphan who was found on a rubbish-heap."

At these words the prince was very angry. "How dare you say such a thing?" he cried. "Remember that I am a king's son and cannot marry anyone but a princess!" With that he commanded his army to follow him and rode off in a huff.

Six months went by, and nothing was heard of the prince or his army. Then one day the bugles were heard in the distance. The queen ran to the window. There was her son coming over the hills, the banners fluttering gaily, the drums beating, the band playing a song of victory. The old man's words had come true—the prince was coming home triumphant.

The queen's heart was not the only one that beat joyfully at the sound of the returning victors. Little Marylka, the prince's adopted sister, was looking out of her window, waving her hand and smiling with delight.

The prince looked up and saw her, but instead of smiling back his face clouded, for he suddenly remembered the prophecy of the old minstrel. One half had come true, and what about the other half?

When he saw Marylka looking from her window and smiling her welcome, he remembered that she had been found seventeen years ago on a rubbish-heap, a poor lost waif. The king and queen had taken her into the palace, and, having no daughter, had brought her up as their own. They loved her very dearly, and so did the prince for that matter, but he could not bear the idea that she was the one he was destined to marry. So his triumphant homecoming was as good as spoilt. Instead of being merry and jolly he was cross and ill-tempered, especially towards his poor little foster-sister.

The time went on: he grew grumpier every day, until at last, from being a pleasant, kind young prince, he became really wicked. And the more he thought about Marylka the more wicked he grew.

One day his heart was so full of pride and anger that he resolved to do a most cruel thing. He ordered a closed boat to be made and put to lie waiting on the river. Then, taking Marylka by the hand, he asked her to go for a walk with him. When they came to the river, he left her standing on the bank, telling her to wait for him. Then he called his servants, and ordered them to put her in the boat and send it drifting down the swift stream.

Marylka screamed and cried, but when she called "Help, Brother!" he called back, "I am no brother of yours,

you miserable foundling," and went away. "Now," he said
to himself, "she is out of the way and I can marry whom I
will."

The boat was carried rapidly down the great river;
Marylka could do nothing to stop it, and no one seemed
to hear her cries. She could not understand why all this
had happened, why the prince had become so unkind, but
she knew she could never go back to the palace, and she
cried bitterly.

At last the boat reached a mill, was caught in the strong
current and carried right under the great wheel. The mill
stopped working, and the miller came to see what had
happened. With the help of his men he landed the boat,
and took poor weeping Marylka into the house. Now
happy days dawned for her again. The miller and his wife
were good people, and when they heard her story, they
gave her a home with themselves.

Several months went by. The old couple became very
fond of their adopted daughter and she of them, and she
was happy, although she could not help thinking of the
good king and queen and longing to see them. And her
heart was sad when she thought of the prince and his
strange and cruel treatment of her.

One day she was picking flowers near the river when
suddenly a hunting party came riding up the road,
headed by a handsome young man. It was the prince.
Before Marylka had time to turn her head he had seen her
and given word to his servants to go after her. But the
country was strange to them and she knew it, so instead
of running for them to chase her she dodged into the
bushes and hid. They rode off in pursuit, but after some
hours spent in vain the prince gave up the chase for that
day. He inquired of the miller, who told him how he had
found her in a boat; but he did not tell him the whole
story as Marylka had told it to him, nor mention that she
had come from the king's palace.

As soon as it grew dark Marylka came out of her hiding-
place, but she knew it would not be safe to return to the

mill, so she began to run as hard as she could. She ran like this for several days, and at last came to a palace. On the terrace she saw twelve princesses sitting and spinning. They were all beautiful and as kind as they were beautiful. When they saw this poor, tired, bedraggled girl, they called her to them, gave her food and drink and new clothes, and asked her where she had come from and why she was wandering about in that forlorn state. She told them her story, and they asked their father to let her live with them. He readily consented and so bright days came to her again. The princesses treated her like a sister, and she in her turn taught them some new embroidery stitches.

All went well until one day a handsome young prince rode up to the door at the head of a large retinue. He had come to pay court to the twelve princesses and to choose one of them for his wife. Poor Marylka at once recognized her cruel foster-brother, and begged the princesses to hide her and to say nothing of her presence in the house. So she was hidden away in a room and the door was kept locked.

When the princesses knew that the suitor was the prince who had treated their friend so badly, they made up their minds that not one of them would marry him. The first day he made love to the eldest. He smiled at her and rolled up his eyes as he made her promises and gave her presents, but it was all of no avail. She laughed at him and mocked him, and at the end of the day, when he asked for her hand in marriage, she said that she was in no mind to marry at all. The next day he courted the second princess, but she mocked him and refused him as her sister had done. The third day he courted the third sister, and so on, until he had been refused by them all.

Now he was furious, and without even saying good-bye he rode away vowing vengeance. In the wood he came upon an old ruined church and a priest living in a hut close to it. An idea then came to him. He told some of his retainers to ride back to the palace, to catch one of the

. . . they had thrown a veil over Marylka's face to make her
more helpless, and the prince, supposing she was one of the twelve
princesses, commanded the priest to begin the service at once.

twelve princesses and bring her by force to the church. Then he bade the priest be ready to perform a marriage service, and so waited.

Now Marylka, having heard that the prince had gone, came out of her hiding-place, and was walking alone in the garden, when all at once some men sprang out of the wood, seized her, and carried her off.

"Have you got her?" cried the prince, as they came galloping up to the church.

"Yes, your Highness," was the answer.

It was growing dusk, the church was dark, they had thrown a veil over Marylka's face to make her more helpless, and the prince, supposing she was one of the twelve princesses, commanded the priest to begin the service at once. Marylka was so dazed that she hardly knew what she did and answered "yes," and "yes," and "yes," and so the knot was tied.

Then they rode in silence to the palace, Marylka in a carriage which the prince had sent for. The king and queen stood at the palace door to welcome the bride. The prince, proud as could be, handed her out of the carriage, the queen's maids lifted her veil—and there, instead of a princess, stood Marylka!

The king and queen were delighted to see again their dear lost foster-child for whom they had mourned as dead. They clasped her in their arms, and in their joy forgot that their son had married a foundling. The prince, seeing it was impossible to go against the decrees of destiny, at first resigned himself, but came afterwards to know that he was the luckiest prince in the world to have won such a wife as Marylka.

And the twelve princesses, who came to the wedding feast with their father, were glad they had acted with so much wisdom and discretion. In fact, there was not a living soul in the country who was sad on that day when the prince married the foundling.

About Jan[1] the Prince, Princess
Wonderface, and the Flamebird

MANY, many years ago there was a king who had three sons. The two elder were bright, intelligent young men, but the youngest, Jan, was considered a dunce and a simpleton. Now all this happened in the days when all people were happy and prosperous, and even the rivers and seas flowed with milk and honey. Therefore, as it may be supposed, the king was a very great man, and had many valuable possessions.

Among other things he had a garden—nay, it was more than just a garden like others, it was a wonder-garden. Everything that grew in it was beautiful, but the most beautiful thing of all was a silver apple tree which bore golden apples.

The king was so fond and so proud of this tree that he went to visit it every day, to gaze on the apples, to touch them one by one, and to gloat over their beauty.

One day he went into the garden, but at the sight of the tree he stood still as if struck by lightning. For what do you think had happened? One of the thousand and one apples had disappeared. The king wrung his hands in despair. Then he called his sons to him and said: "Whichever of you three shall catch the thief who has robbed my favourite apple tree shall be henceforth dearest to me, and I will make him my heir."

----

[1]Pronounced "Yan."

Then the two elder sons stood forth and cried as with one voice: "King and Father, your will shall be done to-day."

"And what say you, my youngest son?" asked the king of Jan the Prince, who stood behind his brothers in silence.

"Nothing, Father," answered Jan.

"You simpleton!" cried his father, looking at him with a frown.

That day the eldest son feasted and drank with his friends. He boasted loudly that he would catch the thief and that he would be dearer to his father than either of his brothers and would inherit the kingdom. By the time he went into the garden to watch he felt stupid and heavy. So after a few minutes he lay down under the tree and fell fast asleep. When he woke up it was morning, and an apple was missing.

The next day the second son feasted and drank with his friends, and, like his brother, boasted loudly that he was going to catch the thief and win his father's favour. But he, too, being tired and heavy, lay down after a very short watch and fell fast asleep. And when he awoke it was morning and an apple was missing.

The third night the youngest son took his place quietly under the tree. He did not forget to make the sign of the cross first on his own brow and then on the tree, and then he watched.

Nothing happened until midnight. Then in the far east he saw a wonderfully bright object come, as it were, out of a cloud. It drew nearer and nearer until at last it reached the tree. Then Jan the Prince saw that it was a wonderful bird with feathers that shone like the sun in the brightest time of the day. The bird was about to take an apple when Jan seized it by the tail. It took fright and flew away, leaving one of its radiant feathers in the prince's hand. Jan the Prince hid the feather in his breast, lay down and rested until dawn. Then he went to his father's palace. As soon as he drew forth the feather the whole

. . . *it was a wonderful bird with feathers that shone like the sun*
in the brightest time of the day. The bird was about to take
an apple when Jan seized it by the tail.

palace and court were filled with a bright light. The king was overjoyed.

"Why, it is the Flamebird's feather!" he cried.

> And then from south to north
> The royal word went forth
> "Whoever brings to me
> The spoiler of this tree
> Whether he be my son
> Or any other one
> The same shall be my heir
> And shall my kingdom share."

Then from all parts of the wide world came knights, lords, courtiers, and gentlemen, and they watched day and night for many months, but the Flamebird came no more. So, seeing nothing was to be done, they all rode off in different directions seeking and inquiring after the bird.

Among them rode the two eldest princes mounted on two beautiful horses, and Jan the Prince on a slow-going nag that stumbled at every step. They rode together for a long way until they came to a cross-road. Here rose a tall cross and on it was written:

> For him who goes straight
> A stick lies in wait
> That will teach him not to make bothers;
> Who goes to the right
> Will end in a plight
> For the evil he's done to others;
> Who takes the left way
> Will oft go astray
> But at last get the best of his brothers.

Now the eldest brother was just going straight on and the second was turning to the right, leaving Jan the Prince the left road, when suddenly, out from behind a hill, a wolf appeared.

He was not really a wolf but a wonder-wolf, but he was so thin and starved-looking that he seemed but skin and bones.

The two eldest brothers shot at him, but whether they had forgotten to load their guns or whether they missed him was never known. At all events, the wolf stood still unharmed, howled at them, and ground his teeth. He looked so hungry that Jan the Prince felt sorry for him, and, taking all the food he had from his knapsack, he threw it to the poor beast. But his brothers went on. Seeing the animal was still unsatisfied and suffering, the prince shot his nag and gave him it to eat.

Then said the wonder-wolf, speaking in a human voice: "Thank you, O Prince. You will not regret having fed me, even though you have parted with your horse. I will serve you better than such a poor beast ever could have done. Tell me where you want to go and why you want to go there."

Jan the Prince told him the whole story. When he had finished the wolf said: "Know, O Prince, that I am no ordinary wolf. I am called the wind-wolf, for I can fly as fast as the wind. Get on my back and hold me fast round the neck, but, whatever you do, don't kick my sides or I'll eat you up."

Prince Jan did as he was told, and in a wag of a tail they were off.

Over meadows and dales, over forests and vales, over rivers and rills, over hillocks and hills, over deep seas and fountains, over oceans and mountains they flew and they flew and they flew till they drew near the far north. There they stopped by a high wall. "Here we are," said the wolf. "The Flamebird is in a garden on the other side of that wall. Go and take it, but I warn you not to take the cage, though it may seem to be more beautiful than the bird itself."

With that he flew away. The prince jumped over the wall, and there was the Flamebird sitting in a cage in the centre of a beautiful garden. As he went to take the bird, the cage, which was set with precious stones, roused his admiration to such a pitch that he forgot, alas! the warning of the wind-wolf and took that too. As he did this, a cord attached to the cage set ringing a loud bell at its other end. An armed guard came running into the garden, arrested Jan the Prince, and took him before the king of that country.

"And who may you be?" asked the king in a fury.

Jan replied: "I am the son of the king in whose garden grows the silver tree which bears golden apples, and I needed to take the bird because he has robbed my father."

"It is lucky for you," said the king, "that he is your father. For the great respect I bear him I will grant you your life and will even give you the Flamebird, but you must do something for me in return. In a certain kingdom there reigns a king who has a horse with a golden mane. He is fleeter-footed than any hare. Bring him here to me and you shall have the Flamebird, cage and all." Whereupon Jan the Prince was filled with sadness, for he had no idea how to set about getting the horse. He went out into the green fields, sat down, and began to weep.

Suddenly he heard a rumbling in the air and, looking up, he saw the wind-wolf flying towards him.

"What is the matter, and why do you weep?" asked the wolf.

"Alas!" cried Jan the Prince, "that I should have been so near happiness and that it should have escaped me!" Then he told the wind-wolf all that had happened.

"You have been very foolish," said the wolf; "nevertheless, I will help you again. I know where the golden-maned horse is to be found. Far away in a distant land, beyond a deep sea and behind twelve locked doors, he stands in a stable. But he shall be yours to-day. Jump on my back as you did before, and hold me tight round the neck, but remember not to kick my sides, for if you do I'll eat you up."

In a wink of the eye they were off.

Over meadows and dales, over forests and vales, over rivers and rills, over hillocks and hills, over deep seas and fountains, over oceans and mountains they flew and they flew and they flew till they drew near the north. And there they stopped by a high wall.

Then the wolf gave Jan the Prince two plants. The first was dream-grass, with which he was to put the guard to sleep. The second was the break-lock plant, with which he was to open the twelve doors.

"But remember, Prince, not to take the horse's bridle, for if you do you will be caught." With this warning the wind-wolf flew away.

Jan the Prince jumped over the wall, waved the dream-grass over the guard until he dropped down in a deep sleep, and then waved the break-lock plant before the first door till the lock fell out and it opened; then before the second and third, and so on till all the twelve doors stood wide open and the horse was within his reach. Now the bridle of the golden-maned horse was studded with precious gems, and was so beautiful that Jan the Prince forgot the warning of the wind-wolf and seized hold of it. Immediately a string attached to it set a loud-sounding bell ringing at the other end, the guard woke up, and the prince was arrested and taken before the king of that country. The king was furiously angry and ordered him to be beheaded, but relented when he saw what a handsome young man the prince was, and he asked him to explain his behaviour. So Jan the Prince related the whole story from the beginning and the king said:

"Well, I will spare your life, but on one condition. In a far-off land beyond the seven seas there lives the youngest daughter of a king, a maiden renowned for her great beauty. Her name is Princess Wonderface. Bring her to me and I will give you not only the golden-maned horse but his bridle too."

Jan the Prince was in despair, and, as before, he sat down in the green fields and wept.

Suddenly there was a rumbling in the air and the wolf appeared.

"What!" he exclaimed. "Weeping again? What is the matter now?"

"Matter enough," said Jan the Prince, and he told the wind-wolf all that had happened.

"Ah, foolish one!" said the wolf, "when will you learn? But I will help you again, for I know how to find the Princess Wonderface. Jump on my back as before, hold tight, and don't kick my sides or I'll eat you up."

In a snap of the jaws they were off.

Over meadows and dales, over forests and vales, over rivers and rills, over hillocks and hills, over deep seas and fountains, over oceans and mountains they flew and they flew and they flew till they drew near the south. There they stopped outside a palace wall.

"On the other side of this wall there is a garden, and there walks the Princess Wonderface," said the wolf. "Wait you here and I will fetch her for you." So saying he stamped on the ground and there stood a splendid young prince. Over the wall he jumped, and there in the garden was Princess Wonderface with her maidens. She thought he must be a guest come to see her father, and was talking to him pleasantly, when all at once he seized her round the waist and jumped with her over the wall, turned back into a wolf and away the three went.

Now the princess, who at first had fainted from fright, came to herself very quickly and fell in love on the spot with Jan the Prince, and he of course with her, for they were both young and beautiful. They exchanged vows of love, and the Princess broke in two a precious ring she wore, gave one half to the Prince as a token and kept the other half herself.

They were very happy, but alas! in time they reached the palace of the king to whom Jan the Prince was to bring her. At the thought of parting they were full of grief. What was to be done? They both began to weep bitterly.

Then the wolf said:

"Now, dry your eyes, you shall not part from each other. I will help you in this way. I will turn myself into the princess and you, Prince, shall take me to the king, leave me there, and then ride away with the real princess." So he stamped on the ground, and there stood a maiden so like the Princess Wonderface that even her parents could not have known which was which. The prince went to the king's palace, gave up the supposed princess, received in exchange the golden-maned horse, bridle and all, and left the king delighted with his bargain. He asked the princess for her hand in marriage, and the wedding was announced for the morrow. The next day the courtiers, lords, and ladies were assembled in the throne-room when all at once the supposed princess turned into a wolf, gave a dreadful howl, and flew out of the window!

Jan the Prince and Princess Wonderface, in the mean-time, were so far on their way, that when the wolf caught up with them they were standing near the palace of the king, to whom the golden-maned horse had to be given up in exchange for the Flamebird.

They were very sad, for they had become fond of their beautiful steed. But what was to be done? The Flamebird must be theirs at all costs, for without it they could not return to the king, Jan's father.

"I see you would like to keep the horse," said the wolf. "Well, so you shall! I will turn myself into his likeness, and you, Prince, shall take me to the king, receive the Flame-bird, and fly with it and the Princess back to your home." So he stamped his foot, and there stood a horse so exactly like the one with the golden mane that nobody could tell the difference. The prince took him to the king, who was delighted, and who gave him the Flamebird, cage and all.

Away rode Jan the Prince and Princess Wonderface, but they had not gone far when the wolf overtook them and told them what had happened. He said that the king, charmed with his new steed, gave orders that the Court should follow him to the forest to hunt. They reached the hunting-field, and the king set off at a gallop in pursuit of a swift-footed roe. Suddenly he found himself riding a wolf instead of a golden-maned horse! In his fright he fell off, and, while the courtiers were picking him up, the wolf flew away. Now having caught up with the prince and princess, as I have said, he took the prince on his back, and with Princess Wonderface on the horse they soon came to the cross-roads where Jan the Prince had first seen the wind-wolf and given him his nag to eat.

"Here we met, Prince, and here we part," said the wind-wolf. "You fed me when I was hungry and I helped you in your need, so we are quits. Good-bye: fare you well, both of you." With that he flew away, leaving Princess Wonder-face and Jan the Prince to pursue their journey on the back of the golden-maned horse. They soon came to the borders of the kingdom over which reigned the father of Jan the Prince. There in a field, sitting under a tent, whom should they see but the two elder brothers, who greeted them with much apparent joy, but who were secretly jeal-ous in their hearts when they saw the Flamebird, the horse with a golden mane, and the beautiful Princess Wonderface. Inviting the young couple into their tent, they regaled them on mead so generously that they both fell into a deep sleep.

Then the brothers thrust a sharp sword into the body of Jan the Prince, and, taking the Flamebird, the golden-maned horse, and Princess Wonderface, whom they had frightened when she woke and forced to be silent, they went to their father's Court. The elder, so they had settled between them, was to have the bird and the horse, and the second brother was to have the princess for his bride.

Jan the Prince lay as dead upon the field. Presently two carrion crows flew down, and were just going to dig their sharp claws into his body, when who should come flying along but the wind-wolf!

"Claws off!" he cried, and seized the smaller of the crows in his jaws.

"Pray, Mr. Wolf, pray spare my child!" cried the old crow, "for it is my only one!"

"I will," said the wolf, "but only on condition that you fetch me some reviving water from the Eternal Mountain."

The old crow flew off, and while he was fetching the

reviving water the wolf made the little crow tell him how Jan the Prince had come to be killed. Now the little crow had been watching from a tree and so could tell all that had happened. Hardly had he ended when the old crow came back, carrying the water in a bladder. The wolf took it and sprinkled it on the body of Jan the Prince, who opened his eyes.

"You have waked me from an excellent sleep," he said.

"An excellent sleep, indeed!" cried the wolf, "which would have lasted for ever but for me. Your brothers killed you and have gone off with your belongings, and the younger is to be married to-day to Princess Wonderface. But I will help you once more. Take this self-playing pipe and this invisible club; go to your father's palace in disguise, blow into the pipe, and see what will happen. Don't forget the princess's ring. I must leave the rest to you." So saying, away he flew.

The prince went to the cottage of a peasant he knew, borrowed his clothes, dressed himself in them, and, going to the palace, slipped into the kitchen. He hid behind the stove, and there watched and listened to what went on. He found that a feast was being prepared for the marriage of his second brother and Princess Wonderface. Before long the king's marshal gave the order that the banquet was to be served at once, and the servants hastened to obey the command. Then Jan the Prince blew into the pipe which the wolf had given him, and immediately, to the most wonderful music ever heard, everything that had life was set a-going. The cook in his apron and cap started prancing, the footmen and kitchen-maids all began dancing, this one with a dish and that one with a platter; and there was a shouting and stamping and clatter, a hopping and dancing, a dancing and hopping, and as long as that pipe played on there was no stopping!

"Spare us! Spare us!" cried the king's marshal, running into the kitchen. "Cease playing, O wonderful musician, and hear the word of the king!" The flute stopped, all the dancers fell to the ground exhausted. Then the marshal announced that the king, having heard from his throne-room the wonderful playing of the piper, begged that he would come into his presence.

"I consent," said Jan the Prince, "on condition that I may drink the health of the bride." This favour was promised, and he was taken to the king.

"Welcome, O great musician!" cried the king. "You have come to cheer us up. For, strange to say, although this is our son's wedding day and therefore a time of rejoicing, we all seem plunged into a deep melancholy. The bride is silent and sad, the Flamebird sings no more, nor flashes its feathers, Golden-mane hangs his head and seems to scent some calamity in the air. We beg you, therefore, O musician, to play your wonderful music and restore our drooping spirits. But first you shall drink the health of the bride."

A goblet of wine was brought to the supposed piper, and as he took it and drank, he dropped into it his half of the ring. Then he passed the goblet to Princess Wonder-face, and, as she drank, the ring touched her lips. She took it, looked at it, and then at the piper, and, recognising him at once, threw herself into his arms. Then the king, too, knew his son, and embraced him with great joy, the Flame-bird began to sing loudly and to flash his feathers, Golden-mane ran out of his stable neighing with delight, only the two brothers did not rejoice, but stood looking dumb-founded and ashamed.

Then Jan the Prince blew into his pipe and at the same time whispered to the invisible club: "Do your work, O club, and punish the guilty ones."

As soon as the pipe began to play, all began to dance—the king, the bride, the courtiers, lords and ladies and gentlemen, and even the Flamebird and Golden-mane joined in with the rest. But not all danced with joy, for the invisible club began to rain blows on the backs and shoulders and sides of the two wicked brothers. They dodged and they wriggled and they tried to get out of the way, but, as they could not see what was beating them so soundly, they tried in vain.

At last the piping ceased and all stood still. The brothers fell on their knees and begged Jan the Prince to forgive them, which of course he did, and there was great rejoicing. Jan the Prince and the Princess Wonderface joined hands and renewed their vows, and the wedding was celebrated that evening. There was dancing, there was singing, bells were clashing and were ringing, and all to their hearts' delight ate and drank the livelong night. I was there, and so can say how gaily passed the time away.

The Old Man's Son

ONCE upon a time in a lonely spot of a dark wood there lived an old man, who had an only son. The boy's mother had died while he was quite a baby, and because no father, however kind and loving, knows just how to wash, dress, and feed such a tiny mite, the old man married again.

The boy grew up to be a fine lad: the father doted on him, and could hardly let him go out of his sight for a moment. Thus he grew up knowing nothing of God's great world—only of the dark forest where they lived.

From the very first the second wife had been jealous of her stepson. She pretended to care for him to please her husband, but in her heart she watched for an opportunity to get him out of the house. When he grew big she set to work to persuade the father that it was very bad for the boy to be brought up in such ignorance and to send him out into the world to learn something. She talked and she talked and always on this same subject, until at last the father decided to send him away. Being an old man now, he was easier to persuade.

So one morning he woke up the boy and said: "It is time, my dear son, that you began to think of earning a mouthful of bread for yourself." Then he gave him a fiddle and a basket of food and led him out into a forest, teaching him to sing and to play a song as they went. When they came to the path which led out of the wood he went aside into a thicket to cut a stick, telling the boy to wait for him. But instead of returning to his son he went home.

The boy waited some time and then fell asleep. When he awoke the sun was low and there was no sign of the father. He called and shouted loudly, but all he heard in response was the twittering of birds preparing to go to bed. So he began to wring his hands and to cry, and to strike his head in despair against the soft mossy ground. But still his father did not come back to him. Then, being hungry, he took out of the basket some bread and a bottle of mead and ate and drank heartily. Then, taking up his fiddle, he began to play and sing an old song that begins

> "Hi, there! you knights
> On the mountain heights!"

and as he played and sang he walked straight before him.

He soon came to the high road. It was still light enough to see the squirrels running up and down the branches of the trees and the woodpecker tapping on their trunks, and from all sides the cuckoo's good-night rang out merrily. In the west the sun was glowing in the midst of what seemed a lake of fire that was reflected in the east behind the dark trees. The whole world seemed to him so joyous and beautiful that his heart swelled with hope and seemed to be laughing aloud. He did not know which way to turn, for every side was so enticing. Suddenly he saw on the ground a huge spider which was trying to kill an ant, also of unusual size.

"Help, help, my good young man!" cried the ant in a human voice. "The time will come when I shall repay you!" The boy at once killed the spider and saved the ant, which started to run off towards the wood.

"Ant, ant," cried the boy, "since you can speak, please tell me which way I ought to go to find the world of living souls."

"Go on straight towards the sun, and you will come to a city where good fortune awaits you," replied the ant, and was out of sight the next moment.

Now the sun disappeared and the heavens were lit by the moon and stars. The boy went on, murmuring paternosters as he went, and chanting and playing. At last he got out of the wood into an open field. In the midst of it flowed a broad river, and beyond it he could see mountains and valleys, and a long, flinty road shone out white in the moonlight. In a shallow part of the river bulrushes grew thickly, and just there he suddenly heard a splash, splash! He ran to see what it could be, and found it was a large fish struggling in a net. It had golden fins, silver scales, and the head and face of a human being. And it called out:

"Oh, good young man, save me! The day will come when I shall repay you!"

The boy waded out into the water, and unfastened the net. The fish sprang out upon the shining ripples and swam swiftly down the current, disappearing in the twinkling of an eye. The boy followed the course of the river on and on. No living soul was anywhere in sight. Suddenly he heard unearthly screams and cries of pain. He ran to the place whence the sounds proceeded, and there he saw two great strapping men dragging an old woman along the ground. When she saw the old man's son she cried out:

"Oh, good young man, save me! These drunken rascals are going to drown me, and for nothing at all!"

"Nothing at all, indeed!" said the men. "Who bewitched my Kasia and the bailiff's wife, eh?"

The old woman swore she was innocent, but in spite of all her protestations they would not let her go. Then the old man's son, taking a great stick in his two hands, fell upon the men and beat them so hard that they, though great and strong, through being drunk had to let go of the old woman and take to their heels.

"May God reward you for your service, young man," said the old woman; "and if ever you should want me you have only to call

> Wonder-woman, come, I pray,
> If you're still alive to-day!

and if I am not with you at once you will know it is because I am dead."

Saying this, she vanished so quickly that, if you had been there to see, you would have thought that the wind had blown her away.

The old man's son went on and on, passing through miles of wild wooded country. The stars began to grow dim, and the eastern sky to glow like a ruby, when suddenly he came upon a young and handsome young man lying flat on his back. He stooped over him and saw that a stream of blood was flowing from a wound in his head, and that he neither moved nor breathed. There was no doubt about it, he was dead, and even St. Stanislaus could not have aroused him.

The old man's son was looking down at him, wondering who he might be, and feeling very sorry for him, when he heard the sound of horses' feet. In a moment four riders rode up, seeking their comrade. When they saw him lying dead the boy so near, they made up their minds that he must be the murderer. So they seized him, and, in spite of all his protestations that he was innocent, they dragged him along the high road to a great city, there to the court before the king, who condemned him to death on the spot, for the dead youth was a great favourite of his. But when the old man's son swore by his soul that he was innocent, the king, being a just man, unwilling to punish if any doubt existed as to the culprit's guilt, ordered him to be imprisoned and put to the test. A bushel of poppy-seeds mixed with sand was to be put before him, and he was to separate the one from the other, grain by grain. This was to be done by the next day if he were innocent.

As the poor lad sat in his cell and looked despairingly at his task suddenly he remembered the ant whose life he had saved, and he called out: "Oh, enchanted ant, come to me and save me from death as I saved you!"

"What I promised I will do," replied a voice from the corner of the cell. The boy looked, and sure enough there was the ant, and crawling after it, through a crack in the wall, were a number of others. They surrounded the plate, on which the sand and poppy-seeds had been mixed, and set to work. In less than an hour there stood a pile of sand on one side and a pile of poppy-seeds on the other, and the ants crawled away through the crack in the wall, leaving the prisoner dancing for joy and calling his thanks after them.

You may imagine the amazement of the jailors when they came to take the condemned youth out to his death next day! They stood as if turned to stone, and then ran off in a body to tell the king. And the king, seeing the hand of God in the miracle, ordered that the boy should be set free, and to make up for the wrong done him he was given a place among the courtiers.

And so fortune began to smile on him; he was happy, and, being bright and intelligent, he learned quickly and grew into a handsome, wise and elegant young man. He found favour with everybody and, amongst others, with the king's own beautiful daughter. The two loved each other dearly, though in secret, as neither dared to show their love openly: for they feared the anger of the king, and that he would banish the youth from the Court if he knew of it.

Time went on, bringing them no hope.

Now the king's castle was of gold, and stood on an island in the midst of a river, casting its glittering reflection on its waters. One day, as he was returning with his courtiers from the chase, his horse reared close to the bridge. The king kept his seat, for he was a good horseman, but his crown fell off and rolled into the river. Lamentations and cries of despair rose on all sides. Not only was the crown very costly, it was precious on another account. For as long as it was in the possession of the king the country prospered and the people knew no hunger, plague, or war, but if it should be lost everything would go wrong. The king turned pale and wrung his hands. Then he ordered that a proclamation should be issued, promising to anyone who would dive to the bottom of the river and bring up the crown whatever he should desire, even if it were his dearest possession.

Many brave young men tried to do this. Some who dived down to the bed of the river never came up again; others returned, but empty-handed. Then the old man's son stood by the river and, thinking of his beloved princess, wished that he could find the crown and so win happiness.

"What is my life without her in any case?" he thought, and he was about to dive when suddenly he heard a splash near him. He looked down, and there was the wonderful fish with the golden fins and silver scales whom he had saved from the net, swimming towards him and carrying in its mouth the king's crown, which it laid at his feet. Before he had time to thank the fish it had plunged back into the river and disappeared.

You can imagine the happy youth lost no time, but in two minutes was kneeling before the king holding the crown in his outstretched hands! There was great rejoicing: the king embraced him and asked what he would have as his reward.

Clasping his sovereign round his knees, the old man's son confessed his love for the princess, and begged that her hand might be his reward. The king sent for the princess and asked her if she would marry the youth. In reply she put her lily-white hand in that of her lover, blushing rosy red as she did so. And then, amidst the beating of drums and the sound of glad music, they were betrothed and the king gave them his blessing.

So everybody rejoiced. The people were glad, because the crown was found and they were saved from misfortune. The king was glad, because he had found a son-in-law who, though not a prince by birth, was a brave young man, evidently beloved by Providence. The young couple were glad, because their wedding was soon to be celebrated. Thus for a whole day there was great merry-making.

But when evening came misfortune again fell upon the Court. The young princess was suddenly taken ill and lay unconscious upon her bed, with cheeks as grey as ashes, teeth chattering, and hot and cold shivers running up and down her spine. The doctors were called in, but all efforts to revive her failed. The king tore his grey hair in a frenzy; the Court was plunged in despair. The princess lay quite still so that everybody thought her dead, though the doctors assured them that she still breathed but was bewitched.

Then the old man's son thought of the old woman whom he had saved, and he called aloud:

> "Wonder-woman, come, I pray,
> If you are still alive to-day!"

Scarcely had he said these words when a gust of wind blew open the window and the old woman flew in on a poker.

"Well, young man, and what can I do for you?" she asked. The old man's son told her all that had befallen him, and she said: "Your sweetheart is not dead but bewitched by a wicked wizard who wanted to marry her himself. He has in his garden a magic plant that grows under the wall and has never seen the light of day. If a leaf of this plant is laid on the breast of the princess she will recover at once, and be healthier than she ever was before. If you wish to get one of these leaves, fly with me to the garden. Get on to the poker behind me, and let us go at once."

They flew out of the window and, carried by the clouds and the wind, they soon arrived at the wizard's garden. Having found the magic plant, the old man's son tore it up by the roots and they flew back with it to the castle. There he bade the old woman good-bye, thanking her heartily for her kindness, and went to his rooms. Here he broke off one red leaf of the plant, and threw the rest into the fire.

Then, going to the princess's room, he laid the leaf on her breast.

As it burnt there was a terrible noise all around the castle, as though the sky had come crashing down upon it, and it lasted till the plant was in ashes. Then, going to the princess's room, he laid the leaf on her breast. In a moment she began to breathe faintly, then she opened her eyes and sat up, looking about her in an astonished way.

What a rejoicing there was now! The king wept with joy, as he saw his dear daughter sound and well again. And the next day the princess was dressed in a beautiful white robe, a wreath of myrtle was placed on her head, and she was led by her maidens to the church, where she exchanged marriage vows with the old man's son, and they lived long and happily together.

The Glass Mountain

LONG, long ago, before ever your greatgrandfathers were born, and far, far away in the very heart of Poland, there stood a glass mountain. It was so high that the top touched the clouds, and on its summit stood a castle, and in front of the castle stood an apple tree, and on the apple tree grew golden apples. And in the castle there was a silver room, and in the silver room a beautiful princess—who was bewitched and kept a prisoner by a wicked sorceress—lived in solitude and sadness. For how could she be happy, although her cellar was full of precious stones and one room in the castle was full of bags of gold, when she could not walk in the sunshine, or hear the songs of the birds, or smell the sweetness of the flowers?

Many brave knights, having heard of the beauty and wealth of the princess and of how she was kept a prisoner in the castle, had tried to climb the mountain and rescue her, but before they could come any ways near the top they fell down the steep sides and were killed. And for nearly seven years knight after knight tried, for nearly seven years the princess watched and hoped that one of them would at last reach the castle and save her. But although they came in hundreds from all corners of the world her hopes were never realised.

Three days before the end of the seventh year a knight clad in golden armour, of whom it was said that he succeeded in everything that he tried to do, rode to the mountain on a splendid charger. The people assembled in the valley marvelled to see how his horse's hoofs trod the glassy slopes as easily as the straight, level road. The knight reached the top and was already close to the apple tree, and the heart of the princess was beating with joy as she watched him from her window, when, behold! a gigantic hawk flew out of the tree and flapped its wings in the horse's eyes. The horse snorted and reared, his feet slipped on the glassy surface, and he rolled with his rider down the side of the mountain and both were killed on the spot.

Two days after this, a student, poor but handsome, strong, young, and wise, came and stood at the foot of the mountain. For a year he had been hearing about the beautiful princess who was imprisoned in the castle and about the knights who had tried to save her, and how each had perished in the attempt. Now he stood looking up at the mountain and at the knight who lay dead in his golden armour with his doughty charger at the foot. He thought for a while as though trying to make up his mind what to do. Then he turned and went into the wood. Here he caught a lynx, killed it, cut off its sharp claws, fixed them on his own hands and feet, and then began to climb the mountain just as the sun rose.

When the poor student had climbed half-way up he began to feel tired and thirsty. A dark cloud floated over his head and he begged it to give him some water to drink. But it passed on without letting so much as a drop fall. He looked up, and in order to see the top of the mountain he had to throw back his head so far that his sheepskin cap fell off. He looked down, and it seemed as if certain death awaited him below. And the sun was setting.

His strength was exhausted: sleep was closing his eyes. He fastened his claws well into the glassy slopes, reclined, and slept till midnight.

The hawk was keeping watch on the apple tree. As the moon rose and threw its light on the shining slopes, the gigantic bird caught sight of the poor student as he lay asleep. It flapped its wings and flew down to destroy him,

. . . the heart of the princess was beating with joy as she watched him from her window, when, behold! a gigantic hawk flew out of the tree and flapped its wings in the horse's eyes.

but just then the student opened his eyes, and when he saw the bird he resolved to make use of its strength to help himself. The hawk grasped him with its powerful claws, but he seized its legs. The startled bird began to soar, and flew up until it was right over the castle. The student looked down. He saw the castle gleaming in the moonlight; he saw the princess sitting in the silver room sighing and dreaming of the knight who might yet save her; he saw the garden and the apple tree shining with its golden fruit. Then, taking his knife from his belt, he cut off the legs of the hawk. It flew screeching into a cloud and so disappeared, but the student fell among the branches of the apple tree. He picked an apple and laid it on the wounds made in his flesh by the hawk's sharp talons: they healed at once. Then he filled his pockets with apples and went boldly to the castle, which was guarded by a terrible and fierce dragon. The student flung a handful of apples at this dragon, and it disappeared in a great fright down the side of the mountain, the castle door flew open, and he found himself in a grassy court full of flowers.

The princess, sitting at her window, saw him coming, and ran joyfully to welcome her rescuer. She gave him her hand, her heart, and all she possessed.

The next day, as he and the princess were walking in the garden, they saw a crowd of people gathered at the foot of the mountain. They called a swallow, and bade it fly down and find out who these might be. What was their joy when they learned that they were the knights who had lost their lives in trying to save the princess! The blood of the hawk, dropping on them, had revived them, and they sent their grateful thanks to their deliverer. And the poor student and his wife the princess reigned king and queen of the Glass Mountain, and lived happily together for many, many years.

The hawk, who was a wicked sorceress, was found dead in a wood.

Thus did a poor student by his wits accomplish what many brave knights failed to do by their strength.